Santa's Story

Will Hillenbrand

two lions

To Dad, who kicked off our holidays by reading
The Night Before Christmas on Christmas Eve,
my favorite tradition.

Published by Two Lions, New York   www.apub.com
Amazon, the Amazon logo, and Two Lions are trademarks of Amazon.com, Inc., or its affiliates.
ISBN-13: 9781542043380   ISBN-10: 1542043387

The illustrations were created digitally.
Book design by Abby Dening
Printed in China

First Edition
10 9 8 7 6 5 4 3 2 1

'Twas Christmas Eve and the outside world was cold and white.

Santa was nearly ready, but the reindeer were
in a world of their own.

Dasher dashed.

"I better hightail it!"

Dancer danced.

Spin, jig, LEAP!

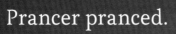

Prancer pranced.

HOO—

Strut, swagger,

HA!

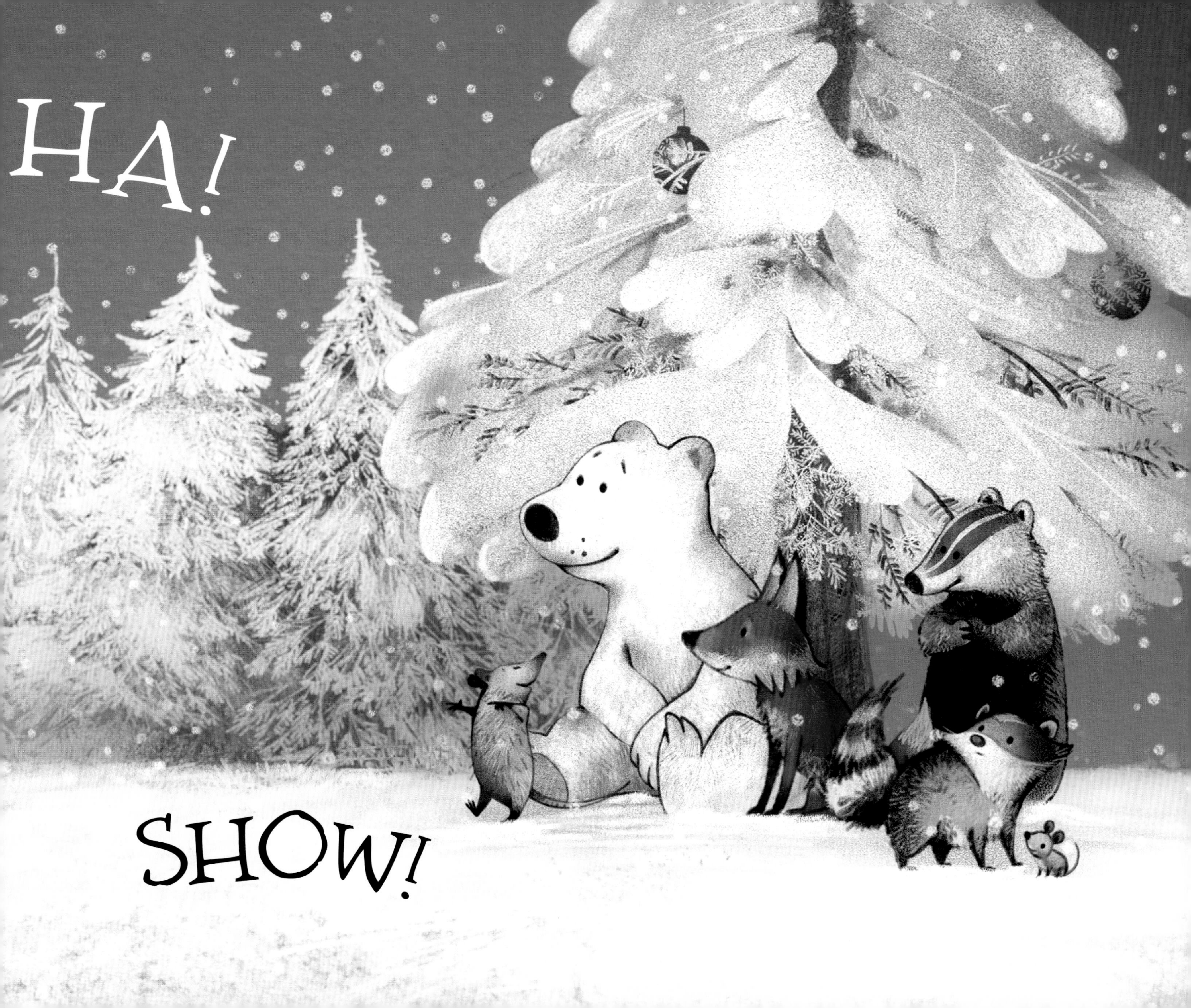

SHOW!

Vixen vexed,

"More snow!"

Comet commented,
"Soon it'll be Christmas!"

WOW!

Cupid crooned,

"It'll be
a kissin'
Christmas!"

Donner dozed.

Zzzzzz . . .

Blitzen boasted,

Santa sighed. "Oh my, I have looked far and wide;
near and far; high and low; here, there, and everywhere. . . .
Did the reindeer disappear?"

Santa decided to play the all-call on his horn.

TOOT,

TOOT,

TOOT...

Still no reindeer.
So Santa rang the sleigh bells.

JINGLE,
JINGLE,
JINGLE . . .

Still no reindeer.
So Santa sang out,

"HO! HO! HO!

Yule deer, please come soon . . .
or we'll be late for Christmas."

Still no reindeer.

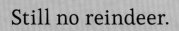

Santa wondered, "Have I overlooked something?"
Then he saw Comet . . . and remembered their
Christmas Eve tradition.

The deer gathered to hear their favorite story.

"'Twas the night before Christmas,

when all through the house . . ."

And when he was done...

Me too.

I was beginning to
think he forgot.

Thanks for reading!

Totally rad.
Good story!
Read it again!
I like the ending.
Now Christmas can begin!

. . . the reindeer were ready.

"Let's bring a merry Christmas to ALL,"

Santa called, "and to ALL a good night."